MARY HOFFMAN is a journalist and writer who has campaigned against sexism and racism in children's literature since 1971. She has written more than 70 books for children. In 1992 *Amazing Grace*, her first book for Frances Lincoln, was selected for Child Education's Best Books of 1991 and Children's Books of the Year 1992, commended for the Kate Greenaway Medal, and included on the National Curriculum Reading List in 1996 and 1997. Its sequel, *Grace & Family,* was among Junior Education's Best Books of 1995 and shortlisted for the Sheffield Libraries Book Award 1996. It was followed by *An Angel Just Like Me, A Twist in the Tail: Animal Stories from Around the World* and *New Born.* Her latest Frances Lincoln books are *Three Wise Women* and *Starring Grace,* a full-length storybook about Grace. Mary is married with three daughters and lives in north London.

JACKIE MORRIS grew up in the Cotswolds and studied illustration at Bath Academy. She has worked in magazine publishing and designed greetings cards for Greenpeace, Amnesty International and Oxfam, and her paintings have been exhibited in Bath, London, and throughout Australia. *Lord of the Dance* (Lion), *Grandmother's Song* and Susan Summers' *The Greatest Gift* (both Barefoot), Anita Ganeri's *Journeys Through Dreamtime* (Macdonald Young Books) and Ted Hughes' *How the Whale Became* (Faber) are some of her most recent books. Her first two collaborations with Caroline Pitcher for Frances Lincoln were on *The Snow Whale* and *The Time of the Lion* – about which Books for Keeps commented, "There is a strength and majesty in the watercolour illustrations which flow across the gutter of the book on every page." Jackie has two children and lives in West Wales.

For Rosie-Louise – M.H.
For my good friends Darren and Steph – J.M.

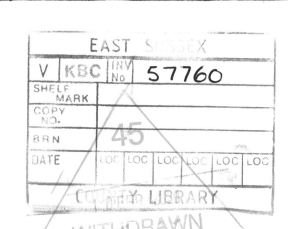

Parables: Stories Jesus Told © Frances Lincoln Limited 2000
Text copyright © Mary Hoffman 2000
Illustrations copyright © Jackie Morris 2000

First published in Great Britain in 2000 by
Frances Lincoln Limited, 4 Torriano Mews
Torriano Avenue, London NW5 2RZ

First paperback edition 2001

British Library Cataloguing in Publication Data
available on request

ISBN 0-7112-1468-9 hardback
ISBN 0-7112-1523-5 paperback

Set in Meridien Roman

Printed in Hong Kong

3 5 7 9 8 6 4 2

MARY HOFFMAN ◈ JACKIE MORRIS
PARABLES
STORIES JESUS TOLD

FRANCES LINCOLN

CONTENTS

❖ INTRODUCTION ❖

Jesus was a wonderful storyteller. He was good at making up stories which were full of things that people of his time could understand. Sheep, grapevines, sowing seeds – these were all familiar to the first people who heard these stories. I am quite sure that if Jesus had been preaching today, he would have told stories about cars and mobile phones and computer games.

A parable is a story with two meanings. There is the surface meaning of what actually happens in the story, and then there is the meaning underneath. Sometimes Jesus told people what he meant by his parables. Sometimes he left them to work out the second meaning themselves. And the meaning is often quite hard to accept.

I have known the stories in this book ever since I was a little girl and I often felt that Jesus was on the wrong side. I was all in favour of the man who was jealous when his brother had a big party thrown for him, or the workers who protested about being paid the same as those who had worked far less than them.

It took me a long time to understand that these are uncomfortable stories and that Jesus meant us to think hard about them. He wanted us to understand that God's law is not like human law. We are selfish and care more about being treated fairly ourselves than about being fair to others.

Some of these parables are still hard for me to understand. But I have never forgotten them, and the images of the house on the rock, the party where nobody came, and the vineyard workers who grumbled about their pay are as much a part of my childhood memories as the home I was brought up in. I hope they will come to mean something important to you too.

Mary Hoffman

A TALE of TWO HOUSES

*Do you like building sandcastles, piling up the
wet sand and patting it with your hands and a spade
to make it strong? But have you noticed how quickly
even the grandest castle crumbles when a big wave comes in?
Jesus told a story about a man who built, not a sandcastle,
but a proper house on the sand. Guess what happened to it!*

There were two men who were building houses for themselves. The first man chose a site on rocky ground. He had to dig very deep foundations to make the house strong. The whole house was solidly built and carefully made.

The man moved in and closed his front door. Not long afterwards, a terrible rainstorm began. The man's roof was well made and didn't leak. The wind blew hard but the windows fitted perfectly into the walls and there were no draughts.

It rained so hard that the rivers overflowed and there was a terrible flood. But the house on the rock stood safely while the rushing flood-waters swirled around and past it. When the storm died down and the sun shone again, the house was undamaged and the man was able to come out and tidy up his garden.

But the second man built his house on the sand. He didn't dig proper foundations, so his house was just resting on the sandy surface. The rest of his workmanship was just as sloppy. The house looked all right from the outside but it was full of faults.

When the rainstorm began, the roof-tiles started to fly off. The windows rattled and the wind got in under the doors. And when the river overflowed, the flood battered at the walls. The house had no foundations to hold it to the ground. The force of the flood water pushed against the house and it started to move. Slowly the walls began to crack under the strain. Then the roof fell in. The whole house tumbled down and was swept away in the swirling waters, along with the man who built it.

Jesus said that the man who built his house upon rock is like someone who hears God's teaching and goes out and does what God tells him. When a man like this is put to the test, his faith holds firm and keeps him safe.

The man who built his house upon sand is like someone who hears God's message but doesn't act on it. When disaster strikes a man like this, he has nothing to support him and he will just collapse.

◆ NEIGHBOURS ◆

*Who is your neighbour? The person who lives next door to you?
Or in the same block of flats? Or in the same street? What about people
who live thousands of miles away? Are they our neighbours too? Jesus told
this story to a clever lawyer who asked him, "Who is my neighbour?"*

Once upon a time there was a Jewish man who was travelling from Jerusalem to Jericho. All of a sudden some thieves jumped out on him. They beat him and took all his money – they even took his clothes. Then they ran away, leaving him for dead.

As the man lay bleeding on the ground, a Jewish priest came along the road. He saw the injured man, but he crossed to the other side of the road and walked on. Next, a Levite came by, another kind of priest. He came over and had a look at the traveller. But he too crossed the road and walked away without doing anything.

The third person to come along was a Samaritan. Now, the Jews and the people of Samaria were enemies. They weren't at war, but they never had anything to do with one another. A Jew wouldn't expect any help from a Samaritan.

But it was the Samaritan who stopped. He went over to the injured man, lifted him up, and stopped the bleeding. He cleaned the man's wounds and bandaged them and took him to a nearby inn. There he paid for a soft bed and food and drink for him.

The next morning, the Samaritan had to go about his business, but he left money with the innkeeper, saying, "Look after this man until I come back. And if it costs you more than I've given you, I'll pay you on my way back."

Jesus asked, "Who do you think was this man's neighbour? The two Jewish priests who walked past him, or the Samaritan?" Well, the answer was as obvious then as it is now: it was the man who looked after him. When Jesus told this story to the lawyer, he meant that our neighbours are not just people who live near us or who look like us or people we approve of. Everyone is our neighbour.

◆ LOST and FOUND ◆

*Have you ever lost something precious? Maybe a toy, or a book,
or a piece of jewellery? Even worse, it might have been your cat or dog
or hamster. Do you remember how you felt when it went missing?
How you searched high and low? And how happy you felt when you
found it again? (And I hope you did.) Jesus told a story
about a shepherd who lost one of his sheep.*

It was quite a big flock – a hundred sheep in all. One day the shepherd was counting them: "Ninety-seven, ninety-eight, ninety-nine..." he said. And then he realised one was missing. Just to be sure, he counted them twice more, in case he had made a mistake. But no. There were only ninety-nine.

The shepherd was frantic with worry. He searched all over the hillside, worrying about the sheep and thinking of all the worst possibilities. "Suppose a wolf has caught her and eaten her!" he thought. "Or maybe she has fallen into the stream and drowned!"

He looked late into the night, ignoring the other sheep, and at last he found the missing one near the top of a mountain. She had strayed far away from the rest of the flock, looking for juicier grass.

How happy the shepherd was! He picked up his sheep – she was quite a small one – and carried her home on his back. And in his heart he was happier about the sheep that was lost and found than about the ninety-nine others who had stayed where he wanted them.

What do you think this story means? Jesus said that God is happier about one person who comes to believe in Him in the end than about ninety-nine people who have believed in Him all along. Maybe that seems unfair to you, but if you remember how you felt when you found the precious thing you lost, perhaps you can understand what Jesus meant.

◆ FAIR PAY ◆

Do you sometimes say, "It isn't fair"? Jesus told a story
which seems very unfair. See if you agree.

There was once a man who owned a vineyard. He grew grapes to turn into wine and every year the fruit had to be harvested. The vineyard owner used to hire men to pick the grapes.

One harvest day, he went out early and found some men who were looking for work. "Would you like to come and pick grapes for me?" he asked. "I'll pay you £50 for a day's work."

The men thought that was fair and agreed to harvest the grapes. They worked hard until midday, and then the vineyard owner decided he needed more workers. So he went out again and found some more men looking for work.

"Would you like to come and pick grapes for me?" he asked. "I'll pay you £50 if you work until the end of the day."

The men were very happy with that and agreed to help harvest the grapes. All the men worked hard, but towards sundown the vineyard owner saw that all the grapes would not be picked unless he employed even more workers.

So he went out again and found some men who had not been lucky enough to find any work all day.

"Will you come and pick the last of the grapes for me?" said the vineyard owner. "There's about an hour's work left and I'll pay you each £50."

The men were delighted and followed him eagerly to the vineyard.

When the sun set and all the grapes were harvested, the owner called the men to be paid. He gave the first lot, who had worked all day in the hot sun, £50 each. Then he called the second lot, who had worked all afternoon in the hottest part of the day, and paid

them £50 each too. Finally he called the last lot, who had worked only one hour in the cool of the evening, and gave them £50 each too.

Well, the ones who had worked all day began to grumble. "It isn't fair," they said. "We've worked all day and yet we only get the same as the men who came for the afternoon or for only one hour." So they got together and went to the vineyard owner. "It isn't fair," they said. "You're paying us the same as the people who worked for only an hour. We should get more than them."

The vineyard owner replied, "Didn't we agree on £50 for your day's work? And haven't I given you that? My money is mine to do what I like with, and it's no concern of yours how much the others are paid."

And then he said a very mysterious thing: "The last shall be first and the first shall be last."

What do you make of this story? It was just as hard for people to understand in Jesus' time as it is now.

But Jesus is challenging our ideas of what fair means. He says that God's idea of fair is letting everyone into the kingdom of heaven, even those who find out about it only at the last moment.

The Jealous Brother

*You know what it's like to feel jealous. It's a horrible feeling,
but everyone has it sometimes. We feel jealous of brothers and sisters
or friends, and we know we shouldn't, but sometimes it's hard not to.
Jesus understood jealousy very well and he told a story about it.*

There was a farmer who had two sons. The older one was steady and reliable and liked working on the farm. He wanted nothing better than to inherit it from his father and carry on working on the land.

But the younger one didn't really like farmwork at all. He was restless and wanted to try another way of life. So he went to his father and said, "I want to try my luck in the city. Will you give me my share of our inheritance now and let me leave home to make my fortune?"

The father was sorry to see his son go, but didn't want to keep him on the farm against his will. So he gave him his share of money and let him go.

At first the son had a wonderful time in the city. He had never had so much money to spend before and he just bought everything he wanted and did everything he wanted to do. He forgot all about making his fortune. Eventually, all his money was gone and he had to look for work.

But work was hard to come by in the city at that time and the young man got hungrier and thinner. In the end he managed to get a job with a farmer, looking after his pigs. But this farm was not the same as the one the young man had been brought up on. The farmer paid him hardly anything and didn't feed him. The young man was so hungry that he started to eat the pig-swill.

Then one day he thought to himself, "What am I doing? I must be mad. The poorest worker on my father's farm has a better life than this. I will go home and ask my father for a job."

The young man walked all the way back to his old home and arrived dusty and with sore feet. He looked like a starving beggar. But his father recognised him from far off and came running towards him. Tears streamed down the old man's face as he embraced the son he thought he'd never see again.

"Forgive me, father," said the young man. "I have wasted all the money you gave me. Would you let me work for you?"

"Work for me? What nonsense!" said his father. "I'm so happy to have you back!"

He took his son into the house and ordered a warm bath for him, and gave him a soft woollen robe and a gold ring to wear. Then he bustled about arranging for a grand meal. He ordered the servants to kill a calf which had been fattened up for a special occasion.

The older brother was hard at work in the fields when he heard the news of the younger brother's return and the celebrations. A frown crossed his usually happy face and he said, "Well, they needn't think I'm coming to their feast." And he stayed out in the field.

The father noticed that his older son wasn't there and went out to find him.

"Come and join in the feasting, my son," he said, "for your brother is home."

"What's all the fuss about?" asked the older brother. "I have been here all the time doing my work without causing you any trouble, and you've never given even a small party for me. My brother has wasted all your money and come back to us a starving wretch, and yet you put on a big celebration for him."

The father clasped his older son in his arms.

"My dear son," he said, "you are always with me and everything I have is yours. But don't you see? It's as if your brother had come back from the dead. Surely that's a good reason to celebrate!"

The story ends there. Jesus doesn't say whether the older brother overcame his jealousy and joined in the feast. But he does say that the younger brother didn't believe himself worthy of the wonderful welcome home he was given.

This is a story about God's love. He is such a loving father that He will welcome back anyone who wanders away from Him. It is like the story of the workers in the vineyard or the lost sheep. And the people who stay true to God all along are like the sheep which didn't wander off or the brother who stayed at home. Sometimes they may feel jealous of the fuss made over the latecomer, but in their hearts they should remember that God loves them just as much. There is enough love to go round in God's world.

SOWING and GROWING

*Have you ever tried to grow a seed? It isn't hard, but you do need
four things – light, air, water and good rich earth. If you plant your seed
outside instead of in a pot, you have to protect it from birds, which like seeds
to eat. When it grows into a little plant, slugs and snails will want to
eat its leaves. And you will need to pull up any weeds that grow near it.*

The farmer went out into his field with a big flat basket of seeds
and scattered handfuls of them as he walked up and down the field.
It was a windy day and some of the seeds were blown outside the
field, because it didn't have a hedge around it. They fell on the road
and birds swooped down and ate them all up.

Some other seeds fell on the stony path around the field. They
started to put down roots, but not very long ones, because of all the
little pebbles in the way. When the hot sun came up, the seedlings
were scorched and shrivelled because they had no water in their
little roots.

Some other seeds fell into a thorny, weedy patch in the corner
of the field. These grew too, but the weeds and thorns grew
faster and took all the water from the plants. The weeds got
taller and the plants died for want of sunlight.

But the seeds that fell on the rich earth which had been dug and made ready for them grew tall and strong. Soon they were a whole field of wheat, ready to be harvested and ground into flour to make delicious bread and cakes.

Jesus went on to explain what he meant by this story. The seed is the message of God's love. When people hear the message, but pay no attention to it, it is like the seeds that fell on the road and were eaten by birds before they could grow.

Other people hear about God's love and seem to understand, but if they don't really believe it in their hearts, they are like the stony ground where the plant can't put down good roots. And the ones who hear the message but forget it, because they are too busy worrying about their problems or trying to make money, are like the patch of thorny ground where weeds choke the plants.

But the people who hear the message and believe it and act on it, by loving other people – they are the ones who are like a field full of wheat, and their goodness shows.

COME to the PARTY

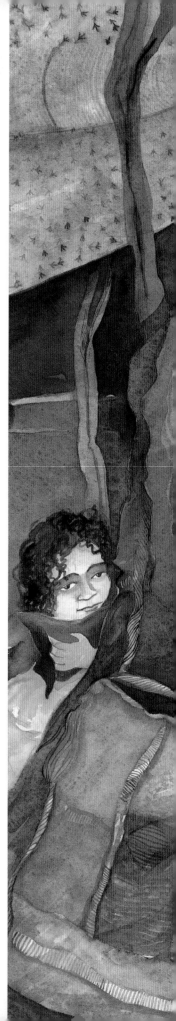

Do you like parties? It can be fun making the preparations, sending out invitations, laying out the food and drink and waiting for guests to arrive. But how would you feel if you did all that and no one turned up? Jesus told a story about a person who had that experience.

There was once a rich man who decided to throw a big party and invite all his friends in the neighbourhood. He gave orders for wonderful rich food and lots of wine to be served.

But when he sent his servants out with the invitations, they came back with a lot of excuses. One man said, "I have just bought a piece of land and I need to go and look at it."

Another said, "I have just bought some animals for my farm and I must go and check on them."

A third said, "I have just got married, and I want to spend the evening with my wife."

The generous host was disappointed. "What is the matter with everyone?" he wondered. "They are turning down a very good party."

He looked at all the food and drink and sent his servants out again. This time they went into town and invited the poor people and those who were blind or on crutches, and they were all glad to accept.

The rich man's dining-room was filling up, but there was still room and plenty of food and drink. So he sent his servants out again and this time they invited the beggars and tramps and homeless people from the streets. You can imagine how pleased they were to be offered a free meal!

All the people who came had a very good time. And not one of them was on the original invitation list.

This story is about people who are too busy to listen to God's invitation to join in his kingdom. Busy people are often concerned about money and possessions and what other people think of them. But God's invitation is open to all. Those people who reply to it will be made welcome. And those who don't turn up are missing the best party in the whole world!

◆ FORGIVENESS ◆

*Have you ever done anything bad? Did you ever have to ask
somebody else to forgive you? Someone once asked Jesus,
"How often should I forgive someone who has treated me badly?"
And Jesus answered the question by telling this story.*

Once upon a time there was a king who had lent money to one of his servants. It was a lot of money – say, £10,000 – and the servant couldn't pay it back.

"Then you must be sold to another master," said the king, "you and your wife and children. And your house and all your goods must be sold too, to pay back the debt."

The servant fell at his master's feet. "Forgive me, lord, for not paying you back. Please don't sell me and my family! It's not their fault. Just give me time, and I will pay back every penny I owe you."

And the king took pity on the servant and said, "I forgive you. We'll say no more about it."

The servant was very relieved. He soon got over his fright and went back to his old ways.

There was another servant who owed the first one a much smaller sum of money – say, £100. The first servant went to the second one and said, "I want the money I lent you. Give it back straight away, or I'll have you thrown into prison."

"Please give me some time, and you'll soon have it all back," said the other man. "Don't make me go to prison."

But the servant was hard-hearted and wouldn't give the other man any time. He had him put into prison.

News of what had happened reached the king and he was furious. He called the first servant to him.

"What about the mercy I showed you when you couldn't pay me back? You should had been just as forgiving to the man who owed you money. Now I shall have you punished, just as I said I would in the first place."

And the king sold the servant and his wife and his children and his house and all the goods he owned, because the servant hadn't shown forgiveness in the way it had been shown to him.

Shouldn't the king have forgiven the servant for treating the other man badly? Perhaps. But Jesus is saying that if we are unkind to other people, we will be judged for it one day. And we will be treated the way we have treated others.

The message of all Jesus' parables is that God wants us to love others as He loves us.

ABOUT the STORIES

*If you want to read any of these parables in the Bible,
this is where to look them up:*

A Tale of Two Houses (The House on the Rocks)
Matthew 7, 24-27; Luke 6, 47-49

Neighbours (The Good Samaritan)
Luke 10, 29-37

Lost and Found (The Lost Sheep)
Matthew 18, 12-14; Luke 15, 4-7
*There is a similar story right after this one in Luke's Gospel,
about a woman who lost a silver coin.*

Fair Pay (The Workers in the Vineyard)
Matthew 20, 1-16
I've changed the Bible amount of one penny to £50 pounds.

The Jealous Brother (The Prodigal Son)
Luke 15, 11-32
"The Prodigal Son" means "the son who wasted his money".

Sowing and Growing (The Sower)
Matthew 13, 3-9; Mark 4, 3-20

Come to the Party (The Rich Man's Feast)
Matthew 22, 1-14; Luke 14, 16-24

Forgiveness (The Unforgiving Servant)
Matthew 18, 23-35

OTHER PICTURE BOOKS IN PAPERBACK FROM FRANCES LINCOLN

AN ANGEL JUST LIKE ME
Mary Hoffman
Illustrated by Cornelius van Wright and Ying-Hwa Hu

"Why are Christmas angels always pink?" asks Tyler. "Aren't there any black angels?"
In this delightfully-illustrated book, Mary Hoffman explores an important question
for today's multi-racial society.

Suitable for National Curriculum English - Reading, Key Stages 1 and 2
Scottish Guidelines English Language - Reading, Levels A and B
ISBN 0-7112-1309-7

THE TIME OF THE LION
Caroline Pitcher
Illustrated by Jackie Morris

At night-time, when Joseph hears a Lion's roar, he decides, against his father's advice,
to go and meet the Lion. He sleeps beside him, meets his brave lioness and watches
the cubs play, learning that danger is not always where you think.
Then one day traders come looking for lion cubs ...

Suitable for National Curriculum English - Reading, Key Stages 1 and 2
Scottish Guidelines English Language - Reading, Level C
ISBN 0-7112-1338-0

STORIES FROM THE BIBLE
Martin Waddell
Illustrated by Geoffrey Patterson

Seventeen lively stores retold from the Scriptures in language children
everywhere will enjoy – a perfect introduction to the Old Testament.

Suitable for National Curriculum English - Reading, Key Stage 2; Religious Education, Key Stage 2
Scottish Guidelines English Language - Reading, Levels A and B; Religious and Moral Education, Levels A and B
ISBN 0-7112-1040-3

Frances Lincoln titles are available from all good bookshops.